Spot's Storytime

Eric Hill

Contents

Spot's
First Picnic

Spot was going on his first picnic with Tom,
Helen and Steve. He was very excited.
"They'll be here any minute, Mum!" he said.
Then Spot had an idea.
"Oh, just what we need for our picnic!"

And before Sally could stop him, Spot pulled the tablecloth off the table – and everything with it. *Crash!*

"Spot!" shouted Sally.

"Oh dear," said Spot.

A knock at the door saved Spot from getting into any more trouble.
"Your friends are here, Spot," said Sally.
Spot rushed to the door.
"Hello, Spot," said Tom, Steve and Helen.

"Oh, great!" said Spot. "Let's go. Oh, I nearly
forgot!" He ran back to Sally.
"Bye, Mum," said Spot. "See you later."
Sally looked up at the sky. It was cloudy.
"Be careful," she said. "And come back if it rains."
"Don't worry," said Helen. "I'll be in charge."

The friends walked up a hill together.
"This is terrific!" said Steve, as they looked at the view.
"I know where there's a big tree by the stream," said Spot. "Come on, I'll race you!" Spot got there first and Steve was second.
"You won, Spot!" said Steve.

When Tom saw the water, he jumped
straight in. *Splash!*
"Oh dear! That was silly, Tom," said Helen.
"You might have hurt yourself."
"Well, I didn't," said Tom. "And I'm nice
and cool now. Let's go and eat."

Spot, Helen, Steve and Tom carefully crossed the stream on stepping stones. Spot put down the tablecloth, then chased Tom around a tree to help him dry off. "This is fun," said Spot.

"Hi, Spot!" Steve had climbed up the tree
and was watching them play.
"This is a great tree," said Steve. "You can
see for miles."
"Come and eat, Steve," called Spot.

Helen unpacked the food and they began to eat.
"It's starting to rain!" said Tom.
"Quick!" shouted Helen. "Under here!" She put
the tablecloth over a branch to make a tent.

"This is a good idea, Helen," said Spot.
They all stood underneath the tablecloth,
but Steve stayed outside.
"It's only a shower," he said.

Suddenly, Steve slipped off the branch and pulled the tent down on top of everyone. They all fell in a heap on the ground.

"You and your tricks, Steve," complained Helen. "We may as well go home," said Spot. So they packed up and started to walk back.

Sally had a surprise ready for them when they got home.

"I knew you'd come back wet and hungry," she said, "so I've made you an indoor picnic."

"Oh, thanks, Mum," said Spot. "That's a really good idea. We're starving."

The friends sat down and ate their picnic. "We didn't mind getting wet," said Spot, "but we did mind eating soggy sandwiches!"

Spot Finds a Key

Spot was in the garden. He saw something
on the ground in front of him.
"Oh!" said Spot. "What's that shining on
the path? It's a key!"

"It's probably the key to the garden shed,"
said a bird.
"Let's see if it is," said Spot.

He tried to put the key in the lock of the garden shed.
"It's too small," said a rabbit.

"Perhaps Dad knows where it fits," thought
Spot. "Oh good, here he comes now."
"Hello, Dad," said Spot. "Do you know
where this . . ."
But Sam was in a hurry.

"Sorry, Spot, I can't stop now. I'm looking for something."
"Oh well," thought Spot, "I'll just have to find out for myself. Maybe it fits Mum's jewellery box."

Spot ran upstairs. He tried to put the key into the lock of Sally's jewellery box, but it didn't fit.

'It's too big!" said Spot.

"I'll try Dad's desk," Spot thought.
He put the key into the lock of the desk
but it wouldn't turn.
"It's the right size," said Spot, "but it
won't unlock the desk."

"I'll ask Mum what the key fits," thought Spot. He went downstairs to find Sally. "Mum," said Spot, "do you know what this . . ."

Sally didn't stop to listen.
"Sorry, Spot," she said. "I must go and help
Dad. I'll be back in a minute."

Spot thought about what else he could try.
"Perhaps it fits the kitchen cupboard."
He put the key in the lock and tried it.

"It goes in the lock, but it doesn't work," said Spot, disappointed. "Now where shall I try?" He thought hard.

"Not upstairs," said Spot. "I've tried there."
Then he saw Sam's tool-box on the floor.
"I wonder why Dad's left his tool-box out?
I'll try the key."

Spot put the key in the lock of the tool-box.
It was the right size and it turned.
"It works!" cried Spot. "It's the key to the
tool-box!"

Spot ran outside to tell Sam.
"Dad!" called Spot. "I've found the key to
the tool-box!"
"That's clever, Spot," said Sam. "We didn't even
tell you that's what we were looking for!"
"Mum," said Spot, "I found the key to
the tool-box!"
"Well done, Spot," said Sally.
"You *are* clever."

Spot Goes Splash!

One morning, Spot woke up to the sound of rain. "Oh dear," he thought. "I'll have to stay indoors today."

"Breakfast time, Spot!" said Sally.
Spot loved breakfast, and as usual
ate it all up. He forgot all about the rain.

After breakfast, Spot looked out of the window.
"Oh good," he said. "It's stopped raining. Can
I go out and play, Mum?"

"All right," said Sally, "but don't roll in the wet grass!"

Outside, the sun was beginning to shine.
Spot stopped and looked up at a rainbow in
the sky.
"That's nice," he said.

Spot walked over to a big tree.
Suddenly he felt drops of water falling on him from above.
"Hello, Spot!" called Steve. He was sitting on a branch and shaking it.
"Stop shaking the tree, Steve!" said Spot.
"You're making me wet."

Just then, Helen came by. She was
wearing shiny red wellington boots
and carrying an umbrella.
"Hello, Spot," she said.
"It's stopped raining,"
said Spot.
"So it has," said Helen.

"You don't need those now," said Spot, looking at her umbrella and wellington boots.
"Yes I do," said Helen, smiling. "I need the wellies to walk through the puddles."

"You mean like this one?" said Steve,
pointing at a big puddle.
Spot ran over and they both splashed in
the puddle, stamping and shouting.
"This is fun!" said Spot. "Oh, you splashed
me, Steve!"

"You two are silly," said Helen. "Now your feet are all wet and muddy."
"We don't care," they both said. "This is fun!"

"It's started raining again," said Helen, "and I'm nice and dry. Bye!" Helen began to walk home.

"Spot!" called Sally. "It's time to come in now!"
Spot ran indoors. When she saw how muddy he
was, Sally was cross.
"Get into the bath at once," she said.

"But it's not bedtime yet!" said Spot.
"I know," said Sally, "but it's time for a bath."
So Spot got into the bath with his toy boat.

"This is fun," thought Spot, as he splashed in the bubbles. "But after this I think I've had enough water for one day."

FREDERICK WARNE

Published by the Penguin Group
Penguin Books Ltd, 80 Strand, London WC2R 0RL, England
Penguin (Group) Australia, 250 Camberwell Road, Camberwell, Victoria 3124, Australia
New York, Canada, Ireland, India, New Zealand, South Africa

First published by Frederick Warne 2007
1 3 5 7 9 10 8 6 4 2
Copyright © Eric Hill, 2007
Eric Hill has asserted his moral rights under the Copyright, Designs and Patents Act of 1988

DVD animation produced in 2000 by King Rollo Films Ltd together with Ventura Publishing Ltd
Music by KICK Productions and Duncan Lamont
Featuring the voice of Jane Horrocks
© Eric Hill/Salspot 2007

ISBN 978 07232 5893 3

Planned and produced by Ventura Publishing Ltd
80 Strand, London WC2R 0RL

Printed in China